TV SAM

Illustrated by Celia Canning

Sam was an actor. He was also a lizard. He lived in a glass cage in Northam Zoo.

Now Sam wasn't just an ordinary lizard. He was a chameleon from the African jungle. A chameleon can change colour without using make-up. Sam could make himself brown,

yellow,

white,

grey,

purple or

green.

One morning, when the children of Northam School visited the zoo, Sam put on a show. He turned himself brown. Then he crawled on to a log, closed his eyes and lay still.

"Where's Sam?" the children shouted. They rushed up to his cage and peeped in.

"Hey, Sam! Where are you?" they cried, peering into every corner of the cage.

"Here I am!" said Sam, opening one eye just a crack.

"Look, he's a branch!" yelled the children. "Oh, Sam! You're so brilliant at acting a branch, we couldn't tell it was you."

Sam was delighted. He loved

having an audience to admire him. He curled up, hooked his tail round a twig and turned green.

"He's changed into a leaf!" gasped the children. "How do you do it, Sam? Come on, tell us!"

But Sam wasn't giving away any

of his secrets. Instead, he dropped off
his twig. As soon as his feet touched
the ground, he turned grey.

"See, he's a stone now!" squealed
the children. They gave three huge cheers
for Sam the stone, making the lizard
house shake.

"Oh, it's fun being an actor!" cried

7

Sam.

He bowed deeply to his audience and waved goodbye as they went back to school.

"I love acting stones and branches

and leaves," he said to himself. "I wonder what else I can do?"

Just at that very moment the zoo keeper brought Sam his food. His arm slid into Sam's cage. On that arm was a sleeve with a small purple button.

"I wonder if I could be a button?"

thought Sam. "It's a difficult part to act, because I'm quite big and that button is small. But I'll try it. A good actor should be able to act lots of different parts."

So, quick as a flash, Sam hopped up on to the keeper's sleeve and curled himself into a button. He made a wonderful button. The keeper didn't even notice he was there. He went all the way home with Sam on his sleeve.

Sam was thrilled. The keeper's

house was full of interesting things he
could act. When the keeper wasn't
looking, Sam slipped off his sleeve.
He turned himself green and tried to
look prickly. Then he jumped into a
pot and sat next to a cactus.

In front of the pot stood a sort of
glass cage.

"I wonder who lives there?"
thought Sam.

The keeper went to the glass cage

and switched on the light. Sam's eyes
nearly popped out of his head. The
cage was full of people, lots of little
people dressed in strange clothes.

"Those are actors!" gasped Sam.

Sam was so excited, he forgot to be

a cactus. He fell out of the pot with a thump. The keeper heard the noise and turned round.

"It's Sam!" he cried. "Come back, Sam!"

He bent down to grab Sam, but Sam dodged out of his way just in time. The keeper grabbed a handful of prickly cactus instead!

Sam rushed out of the house and

jumped on to the window sill next door. The keeper rushed out after him, but all he saw were two snails. He raced off down the road.

As soon as the keeper had gone,

one snail on the window sill moved
and uncurled. It was Sam all the time.
Sam had been acting the part of a
snail.

As Sam stretched himself out,

he heard a noise in the room behind him. He peeped through the window and saw another glass cage with the light on. On this cage it said "BBC" in big letters.

Sam wondered what the letters meant. As he was wondering, he saw the letters again—only this time they were written backwards as a reflection in the window glass. Sam turned round and saw a bus pass by. On the front of it, where it tells you where the bus is going, were the letters "BBC".

Sam ran to the bus stop. There was

no time to lose. He had no money to pay, so he jumped on to a little girl's shoulder and sat on her head.

"That's a smart pair of earphones

you're wearing," said the conductor
to the girl.

"Pardon?" said the girl. She could
not hear because Sam was curled
round her ears.

The bus drove off and stopped at a

21

building with the letters "BBC" on it.

The little girl felt a tickle in her ear.
It was Sam saying "Thank you" and
"Goodbye". He jumped off her head
and ran straight towards the BBC
building.

"Hello!" he yelled as he skidded in

through the door. "Can I be an
actor?"

The BBC doorman came running.

"Who said that?" he demanded.

"I did," squeaked a voice from the
floor.

The doorman looked down. All he

saw was a large purple hairbrush. It was Sam. He was acting again.

The hairbrush got up.

"Please," begged Sam. "I want to be an actor in a glass cage. Will you help me?"

"A glass cage?" said the doorman, scratching his head in amazement. "I've never heard of such a thing."

"But you must have!" cried Sam. "There's one in that room over there."

Sam pointed at the doorman's own

private room. The doorman turned and stared. A big grin spread over his face.

"That's not a glass cage," he chuckled. "That's a television set."

"I want to be an actor in a television set then," said Sam, jigging up and down with excitement. "How do I get inside?"

The doorman coughed to stop himself laughing. He picked Sam up and looked him straight in the eye.

"You don't understand, do you, young fellow?" he said. "You don't have to get inside a television set. That's just a picture. I'll show you."

The doorman carried Sam down a

corridor. They came to a door with a small round window in it. Sam peeped through the window at a room filled with cameras. Sam was used to seeing cameras at the zoo, but these were much bigger.

"That room is a studio," said the doorman. "Those cameras are getting ready to film an adventure story. It's called *'The Pirates of Shark Bay'*."

"Where are the actors?" whispered Sam. His heart was thumping so much he could hardly speak.

"Here they come!" said the doorman.

Sam heard laughing and shouting.

He pressed his nose against the
window. At the far end of the studio
there were heaps of sand and some
cardboard waves. Into the middle of
the sand marched a band of fierce ruthless
pirates with parrots on their shoulders.
Sam trembled with delight.
He wanted to be a fierce ruthless
pirate too!

"Please!" he squealed in the

doorman's ear. "Please, please tell me how I can be a pirate."

"A pirate?" said the doorman. He giggled to himself. Who ever heard of a lizard pirate? But he didn't want to disappoint Sam. "If you want to be a pirate," he said, "try that lady over there." He pointed to a lady with a clipboard who was telling the pirates what to do. "She's the producer and she's in charge here."

"Thank you," said Sam. He jumped out of the doorman's arms and barged in through the door.

The producer was busy. She was

flicking the papers on her clipboard
and looking rather worried. Sam crept
up behind her. He turned brown,
closed one eye and stood on one leg.

"Yo-ho-ho!" he yelled in a very
fierce voice.

Sam startled the producer so much

that she leapt in the air. She was very
surprised, but she didn't seem annoyed.

"A pirate!" she gasped. "A
PIRATE! Where did you come from?"

"From the zoo," chuckled Sam.
"I'm Sam the chameleon and I want
to act the part of a pirate."

"What luck!" cried the producer.
"I could do with an extra pirate for my
show. Wait here while I get you a
parrot."

Sam was thrilled. He practised his

33

"Yo-ho-hos" while the producer
rushed to fetch a large African parrot.

"Every pirate has to have a parrot
on his shoulder," she said. "This
parrot's for you."

"Hooray!" said Sam. He was sure
he'd look great with a parrot.

But as soon as the parrot sat on his
shoulder, Sam fell over!

The producer groaned and helped
Sam to his feet.

"Oh dear!" she said. "You're too
small to be a pirate. What a shame!"

Sam clung to her tightly. He'd just

had another idea.

"Can I be a parrot then?" he
squeaked. "I'd make a wonderful
parrot. Watch me. I don't even need
make-up."

The producer gasped in surprise. Sam's
head had turned purple. His
back had turned yellow and his tail
was bright green.

"Brilliant!" she said. "You're the

most colourful parrot I've ever seen."

"Pretty Polly!" squawked Sam.

"Pooh!" said the real parrot.

The real parrot flew up in the air
and flapped his wings in Sam's face.

"Oh, gosh!" sighed the producer.
"I've just remembered. You can't fly,
Sam, so you can't be a parrot. I'm sorry."

"But I've got to be something,"

37

wailed Sam. "If I can't fly, I'll try
swimming."

Sam dashed across the studio floor and
plunged into the middle of the cardboard
waves. He folded his long tongue into lots
of sharp triangles like teeth.

"Look at me!" he yelled. "I'm the
shark of Shark Bay!"

The pirates took one look at Sam
and trembled all over. But they
weren't trembling with fright. They
were laughing! They just couldn't
help it. The waves were so big and
Sam was so small. He didn't look
scary at all.

Even the producer was laughing.
She plucked Sam from the sea and patted

him kindly.

"Hard luck, Sam!" she said, swallowing hard to stop herself giggling. "There's no part to suit you in *'The Pirates of Shark Bay'*. I'm afraid you'll have to go back to the zoo."

"But there must be a part for me somewhere," cried Sam. "I'm such a wonderful actor!"

The producer shook her head. Sam's chin flopped on to his chest.

"Poor Sam!" said the pirates.

Sam crept sadly away with his tail between his legs. Out of the studio he

went and down the long corridor. A door burst open in front of him, but Sam hardly noticed. Through the door rushed another sad person. It was the BBC weather man.

"Oh dear! Has anyone seen my clouds?" wailed the weather man.

"I've lost all my clouds. We're on the air and I've got nothing to put on my weather map. What shall I do?"

Just then he saw Sam with tears on his cheeks. Sam looked just like a rain cloud!

The weather man grabbed him. He rushed to put Sam on his map. Sam opened one eye and saw cameras pointing at him.

"I'm on telly!" he gasped.

"You're a cloud!" whispered the

weather man.

"A cloud!" squeaked Sam. "I'm brilliant at acting clouds. Watch this."

Sam really was brilliant!

He moved across the map without any help. In the South he was grey.

In the East he turned white.
In the North and West he was a

round yellow sun.

"What a wonderful cloud!" gasped
people all over the land. "That cloud

can change colour!"

"It's Sam!" yelled the children from
Northam School. "That cloud must

be Sam!"

So now Sam doesn't have to go
back to the zoo. He's a star!

Have you seen him? Watch carefully. If there's a cloud on your telly that moves, changes colour, and sometimes pretends it's a pirate — that's Sam!